Jean and Claudio Marzollo

Blue Sun Ben

PICTURES BY
Susan Meddaugh

Dial easy-to-read

DIAL BOOKS FOR YOUNG READERS
E. P. Dutton, Inc.   NEW YORK

WITHDRAWN

For Susan Jeffers and Rosemary Wells
J.M. and C.M.

For H.
S.M.

Published by
Dial Books for Young Readers
A Division of E. P. Dutton, Inc.
2 Park Avenue
New York, New York 10016

Published simultaneously in Canadà by
Fitzhenry & Whiteside Limited, Toronto

Library of Congress Cataloging in Publication Data
Marzollo, Jean. Blue Sun Ben.
Summary: In a world of two suns Ben, who is a boy
during Red Sun and a chipmunk during Blue Sun, falls
into the clutches of the Animal Singer, an evil man
who changes people and animals into shapes to suit
his own purposes.
[1.Fantasy.] I.Marzollo, Claudio.
II.Meddaugh, Susan, ill. III.Title
PZ7.M3688Bl 1984 [E] 83-18808
ISBN 0-8037-0056-3
ISBN 0-8037-0063-6 (lib. bdg.)

First Edition
(COBE)
10 9 8 7 6 5 4 3 2 1

The art for each picture consists of
a pencil drawing and two pencil overlays
reproduced in black, red, and blue halftone.

Reading Level 2.1

CONTENTS

LATE FOR HOME

Ben lived in a world
with two suns.

When the Blue Sun was up,
Ben was a chipmunk.

When the Red Sun was up,
he was a boy.

Everyone in his world was like that.

His mother always told Ben

to come home to change shape.

But one night Ben was late.

He had stayed out too long.

His mother would be mad.

No matter how fast Ben ran,

he would never get home on time.

There was only one hope.

He could cut across Owl Hill.

That was dangerous

because the giant owl might see him.

Lately the owl had caught

many small animals at sun change.

Ben was afraid,

but he took the short cut anyway.

He ran as fast as he could

and then even faster.

He was almost on the other side
when something grabbed him.
Ben felt himself being lifted
up, up, up into the sky.
Claws dug into his back.
Then suddenly they let him go.

Ben landed hard on a mountain ledge.
Standing over him was the giant owl
with his mouth wide open.
Ben was terrified.
"Please, don't eat me!" he begged.

But the owl was only yawning.

"I'm not ready for you yet,"

said the owl.

He put his wing over Ben

and started to snore.

Ben peered out between some feathers

and saw the Blue Sun sink in the sky.

THE MAN IN THE CAVE

By the time the Red Sun rose,

Ben had changed into a boy.

When he awoke, he saw a cave.

Inside a man with big eyes

was mixing powders and liquids.

Where was the owl?

Suddenly Ben knew what had happened.

The owl was really the Animal Singer!

Ben had heard of this evil man,

who lived in a mountain cave.

He could change people and animals

into whatever shapes he wanted,

and they could not stop him.

Now he was singing in a nasty voice.

"Little chipmunk

That I hold,

This will turn you

Into gold!"

The man slammed down his spoon.

"It's still not right," he said.

Ben gasped in horror.

The Animal Singer heard him!

"Get over here," he said.

"Move these stones out of the cave."

The Animal Singer went back to work.

Quickly Ben moved the stones outside.

He was afraid not to.

"Quiet!" shouted the man.

"I must not be disturbed!"

Ben carried the stones on tiptoe.

Soon he had made a big pile.

Ben was very tired.

He put a big round rock on top

and sat down for a minute to rest.

"Ouch!" said someone.

Ben looked around in fear.

The Animal Singer was still inside.

"Who said that?" whispered Ben.

"Me," the voice said.

"Come out from behind the stones,"
said Ben.

"I can't," said the voice.

"Why not?" asked Ben.

"Because I *am* a stone," said the voice.

"What do you mean?" asked Ben.

The voice answered,

"The Animal Singer is trying

to turn animals into gold.

But his magic isn't working,

so he turns us into stones.

We were all alive once.

I was a rabbit.

He made an extra mistake with me.

That's why I can talk.

Listen, I'll tell you how to escape."

THE STONE'S PLAN

Just then the Animal Singer

came out of the cave.

"Too tired to work?"

he asked.

"No!" said Ben, jumping up.

"I love to work!

I'll clean up your whole cave!

Don't mind me!"

Ben hurried into the cave

and got more stones.

When the Animal Singer

was busy with his powders and liquids,

Ben went back to talk to the stone.

"Here's what you do," said the stone.

"Wait until Blue Sun.

You'll be a chipmunk then.

Slip out from under the owl's wing

and run toward the back of the cave.

There you'll see a little tunnel."

"Where can I go for help?" asked Ben.

"Find a girl named Kiri.

She tricked the Animal Singer once.

He talks about her all the time.

He hates her," said the stone.

"Kiri Bluebird?" asked Ben.

"Yes," said the stone.

"Do you know her?"

24

"She's my cousin!" said Ben.

When the Red Sun began to set,

the Animal Singer and Ben lay down.

Ben was terrified.

What if he slept too long

and could not escape?

But he did not have to worry.

The Animal Singer snored

like a machine gun.

At Blue Sun, Ben was wide awake.

By this time he was a chipmunk,

and the Animal Singer was an owl.

Ben slipped out from under his wing

and fled to the back of the cave.

FOX WOMAN

Kiri's house was far away.

By the time Ben got there,

it was Red Sun.

He was a boy again.

"Ben!" cried Kiri.

"What are you doing here?
Your mother is so worried!"
Ben told her everything.
"We need the fox woman," said Kiri.
"She's the one who helped me
trick the Animal Singer.
Come, let's go quickly
before my parents stop us.

We'll tell them everything later."

Ben and Kiri ran into the desert

and found the fox woman's den.

She gave them mint tea

and listened to Ben's story.

"That idiot," she said angrily.

"He never uses his magic properly.

All he ever thinks of is himself.

Animals into gold, indeed!

This time he has asked for it.

I have a plan.

Hold my hands and shut your eyes."

Ben and Kiri did as they were told.

They felt a rush of cool wind

and then a sudden flash of heat.

When they opened their eyes,
they were at the mountain.

Above them they could hear

the Animal Singer yelling on his cliff.

"Where is that chipmunk boy?

My new formula is ready.

This time I know it will work!"

Carefully the fox woman sprinkled

red powder in a circle on the sand.

"Ben, you stand in this circle.

Call up to the Animal Singer

and make fun of him.

He will come down to get you,

but don't move until I say, 'NOW!'

Can you do this?

You must be very brave."

Ben nodded, although he was afraid.

The fox woman and Kiri hid.

Ben got in the circle.

"Yoo-hoo, Animal Singer," he called.

"Lose anything?"

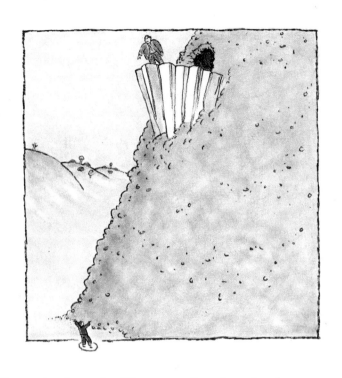

The Animal Singer looked down.

"Chipmunk boy!" he screamed.

"Did you think you escaped from me?

Don't you know

I can change my shape

whenever I want?"

CLAWS IN THE SAND

Instantly the Animal Singer changed
into the giant owl.

Screaming with horrid laughter,
he flew down over Ben.

Ben almost ran but he didn't.

Instead, he looked up at the owl

and stuck his tongue out.

"Fool!" the owl screeched.

Down, down, he came

with his claws stretched out

like knife points.

"NOW!" yelled the fox woman.

Ben made the biggest leap

he ever had.

As he did,

the owl's claws hit the sand.

He tried to fly away,

but his claws were stuck.

"Help!" the owl screamed.

He could not pull his claws out.

Deeper and deeper

they sank into the ground.

Ben stopped running and looked back.

Kiri and the fox came out of hiding.

The fox woman gave Kiri

a ruby necklace

and told her to aim it at the owl.

Zap! Red lightning hit him,

and the owl began to change.

His feathers turned to leaves.

His legs turned to bark.

His claws became roots.

The owl turned into a big old tree growing in the sand.

"That will hold him for a while,"
said the fox woman.
"Now aim the ruby at the mountain."
Red lightning flashed again,
and stones fell down the mountain.
As they hit the ground,
they turned into children.

A boy with a round face hugged Ben.

He seemed familiar.

"Remember me?" he asked.

"I was the talking stone!"

"Hush, everyone," said the fox woman,
pointing to the setting red sun.
"It's time to lie down."
And so they did.

Children of all sizes and shapes
lay down and fell asleep.
There were so many of them!
They stretched out everywhere.

When the Blue Sun rose,

animal sounds filled the air.

There was chirping and tweeting,
meowing and croaking.

But all the sounds

meant the same thing:

HOME!

"Come on, Kiri," said Ben.

"Let's go home too!"

47186

E
M

Marzollo, Jean

Blue Sun Ben

$8.89

DATE		
FEB 2 4 1987		
MAR 1 0 1987		
APR 2 1987		
MAY 8 1987		
MAY 2 1 1987		
JUN 9 1987		
JUL 0 1 1987		
JUL 3 0 1987		
AUG 1 3 1987		
AUG 3 1 1987		

WITHDRAWN

×